NAME YOUR EMOTIONS

SOMETIMES I FEEL CONFUSED

by Jaclyn Jaycox

PEBBLE
a capstone imprint

Published by Pebble, an imprint of Capstone.
1710 Roe Crest Drive, North Mankato, Minnesota 56003
capstonepub.com

Library of Congress Cataloging-in-Publication Data
Names: Jaycox, Jaclyn, 1983- author.
Title: Sometimes I feel confused / Jaclyn Jaycox.
Description: North Mankato, Minnesota : Pebble, [2022] | Series: Name your emotions | Includes bibliographical references and index. | Audience: Ages 5-8 | Audience: Grades K-1 | Summary: "What does it mean to be confused? Confusion may not make us feel good, but it's an emotion everybody has! Children will learn how to identify when they are confused and ways to manage their feelings. Large, vivid photos help illustrate what confusion looks like. A mindfulness activity will give kids an opportunity to explore their feelings"— Provided by publisher.
Identifiers: LCCN 2021029769 (print) | LCCN 2021029770 (ebook) | ISBN 9781663972248 (hardcover) | ISBN 9781666326116 (paperback) | ISBN 9781666326123 (pdf) | ISBN 9781666326147 (kindle edition)
Subjects: LCSH: Uncertainty—Juvenile literature.
Classification: LCC BF463.U5 J46 2022 (print) | LCC BF463.U5 (ebook) | DDC 153.4/2—dc23
LC record available at https://lccn.loc.gov/2021029769
LC ebook record available at https://lccn.loc.gov/2021029770

Image Credits
Capstone Studio: Karon Dubke, 9, 11, 17, 19; Dreamstime: Paulus Rusyanto, 21; Getty Images: DragonImages, 7; Shutterstock: Color Symphony, Design Element, Anatoliy Karlyuk, Cover, CGN089, 8, PR Image Factory, 18, sirikorn thamniyom, 15, Tyler Olson, 5, YAKOBCHUK VIACHESLAV, 13

Editorial Credits
Editor: Erika L. Shores; Designer: Dina Her; Media Researcher: Jo Miller; Production Specialist: Tori Abraham

Printed and bound in the USA. PO4608

TABLE OF CONTENTS

Words in **bold** are in the glossary.

WHAT IS CONFUSION?

Imagine you are in school. Your teacher writes a math problem on the board. You have never seen a problem like that before! You don't know how to even begin to **solve** it. You might be feeling confused.

Confusion is an **emotion**, or feeling. You can have many different emotions every day.

WHAT DOES IT FEEL LIKE TO BE CONFUSED?

Can you think of a time you felt confused? Maybe you were learning a new song on the piano. How did you feel?

When you are confused, you may not think clearly. It can feel like all your thoughts are mixed up. It can be hard to pay attention. You might feel nervous or **anxious**.

USING YOUR SENSES

Everyone has five **senses**. People can touch, taste, and hear. They can see and smell things too. Your senses send messages to your brain. That's where feelings start.

Have you ever heard a noise, but aren't sure where it came from? Or eaten something that tasted much different than you expected? These things probably made you feel confused.

TALKING ABOUT YOUR FEELINGS

Talking about your feelings is important. It can be hard to sort out your feelings alone. Talking to someone about them can help. If you feel confused, tell someone you care about and trust. They can try to help you with your problem. You will feel better too!

UNDERSTANDING CONFUSION

Confusion happens when you are unsure about something. Maybe someone you love suddenly got very sick. You might be confused about what's happening.

Confusion can make you feel uncomfortable. Sometimes it can even make you feel embarrassed. You might think you are the only one feeling confused. But most likely you are not alone!

Confusion can be a helpful emotion. It makes you think. It challenges you. Think about the new math problem on the board. You want to make sense of it. Sometimes your best thinking happens when you are confused. You learn how to be a problem-solver.

HANDLING YOUR FEELINGS

Everyone feels confused sometimes. It's part of growing and learning. Confusion can come with new experiences. It's how you handle it that matters.

Confusion can make you want to run away. You might try to avoid things that make you feel this way. But you can turn that feeling into something **positive.**

Be patient with yourself. If something is confusing you, take a deep breath. Give yourself a few minutes to gather your thoughts. Maybe writing things down helps them to make sense.

Take a break. Play outside or read
a book. Clear your mind and come back
to it later. Everyone does things
differently. It can take time to find
your own special way!

MINDFULNESS ACTIVITY

Superheroes have strong senses. Try this activity to test your superhero senses!

What You Do:

1. Take a few deep breaths. Close your eyes.

2. What can you hear? What can you smell?

3. Now open your eyes. What can you see?

4. Slowly walk around the room.

5. What can you feel? Is there anything you can taste?

Tuning in to your senses will help calm you. Your confusion will melt away in no time.

GLOSSARY

anxious (ang-SHUSS)—worried or fearful

emotion (i-MOH-shuhn)—a strong feeling; people have and show emotions such as happiness, sadness, fear, anger, and jealousy

positive (POS-i-tiv)—helpful or upbeat

sense (SENSS)—a way of knowing about your surroundings; hearing, smelling, touching, tasting, and sight are the five senses

solve (SOLV)—to find the answer to a problem

READ MORE

Christelis, Paul. *Exploring Emotions: Everyday Mindfulness*. Minneapolis: Free Spirit Publishing, 2018.

Llenas, Anna. *The Color Monster: A Story About Emotions*. New York: Little, Brown and Company, 2018.

INTERNET SITES

KidsHealth: Talking About Your Feelings
kidshealth.org/en/kids/talk-feelings.html

PBS Kids: Draw Your Feelings
pbskids.org/arthur/health/resilience/draw-your-feelings.html

INDEX

ABOUT THE AUTHOR

Jaclyn Jaycox is a children's book author and editor. When she's not writing, she loves reading and spending time with her family. She lives in southern Minnesota with her husband, two kids, and a spunky goldendoodle.